I See a Cat

I See a Cat

PAUL MEISEL

I Like to Read®

HOLIDAY HOUSE • NEW YORK

I Like to Read® books, created by award-winning
picture book artists as well as talented newcomers,
instill confidence and the joy of reading in new readers.

We want to hear every new reader say, "I like to read!"

Visit our website for flash cards, activities, and more about the series:
www.holidayhouse.com/I-Like-to-Read/
#ILTR
This book has been tested by an educational expert
and determined to be a guided reading level A.

Copyright © 2017 by Paul Meisel
All Rights Reserved
HOLIDAY HOUSE is registered in the U.S. Patent and Trademark Office.
Printed and bound in March 2017 at Tien Wah Press, Johor Bahru, Johor, Malaysia.
The artwork was created with watercolor, acrylic, and pencil on
Strathmore paper with digital enhancement.
www.holidayhouse.com
1 3 5 7 9 10 8 6 4 2
Library of Congress Cataloging-in-Publication Data is available.

ISBN 978-0-8234-3680-4 (hardcover)
ISBN 978-0-8234-3849-5 (paperback)

For Marcia, Tim and Jeanne,
dog lovers all

I see a cat.

I see a bird.

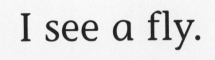

I see a fly.

I see a squirrel.

WOODSON

I see mice.

I see a bee.

I see a squirrel.

I see a boy.

I see a squirrel.

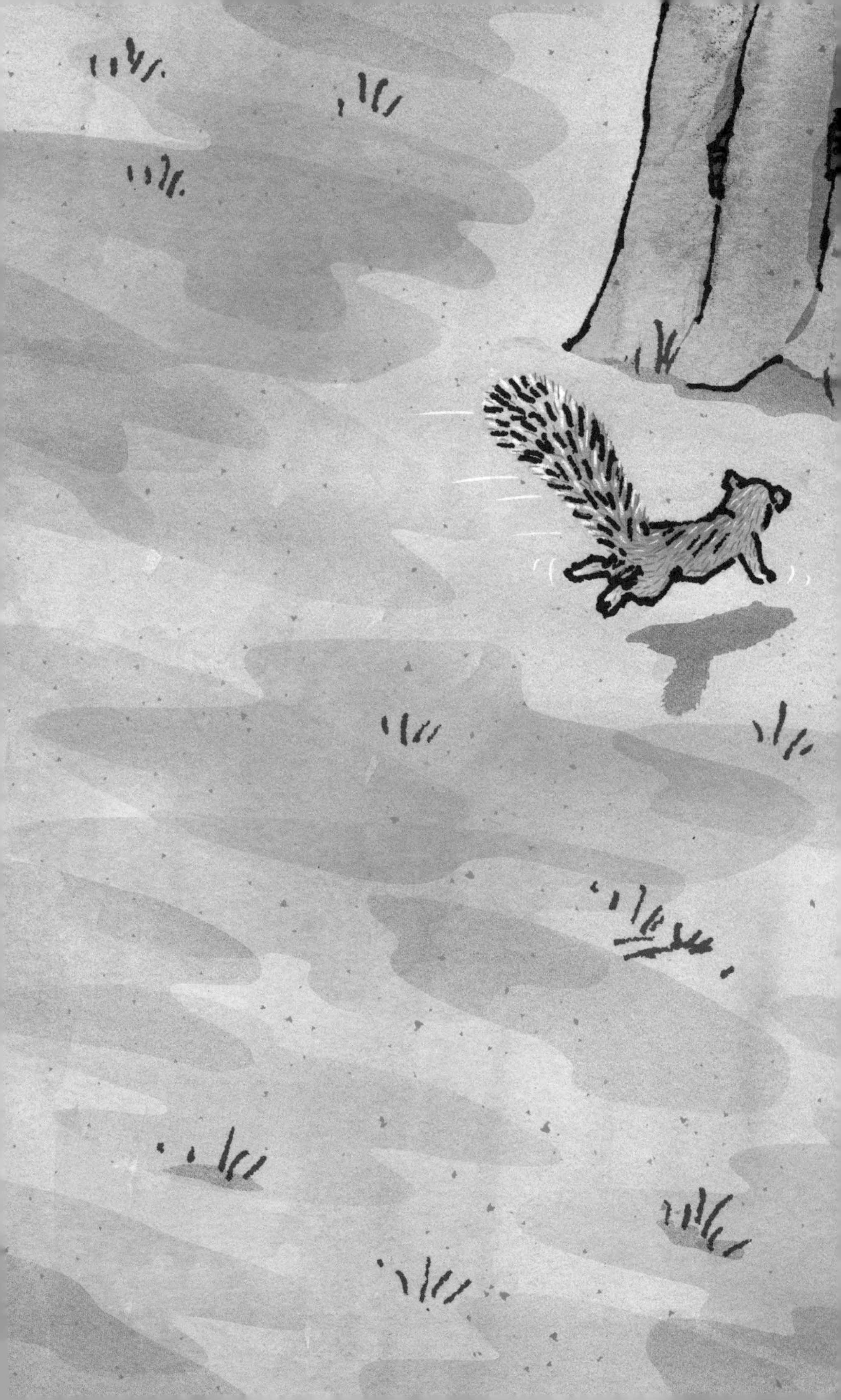

I Like to Read®

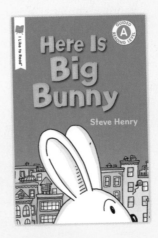

Visit http://www.holidayhouse.com/I-Like-to-Read/ **for more about I Like to Read®**
books, including flash cards, reproducibles, and the complete list of titles.